# Table of Contents

| | |
|---|---|
| What Do Cheetahs Do? | 3 |
| Photo Glossary | 15 |
| Index | 16 |
| About the Author | 16 |

# Can you find these words?

gazelle

marks

prey

tail

# What Do Cheetahs Do?

Cheetahs are big African cats.

Cheetahs have **marks** on their fur.

See the lines from eyes to mouth?

Cheetahs balance with the help of a long **tail**.

tail

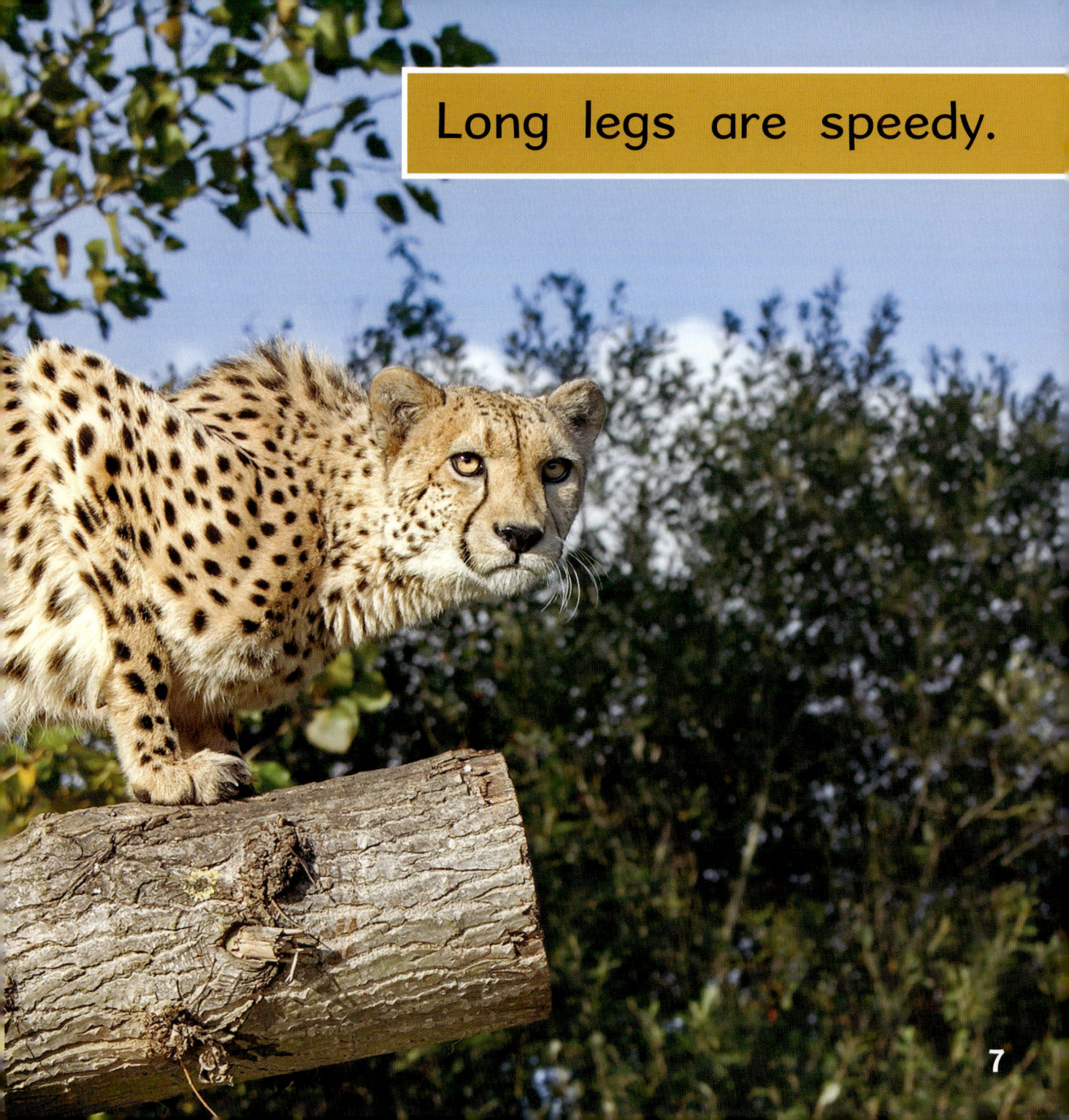
Long legs are speedy.

Cheetahs run!

They are the fastest land animals.

Cheetahs see well!

prey

Their eyes spy **prey.**

Cheetahs hunt by day.

They may catch a rabbit, a warthog, or a **gazelle**.

gazelle

# Did you find these words?

They may catch a rabbit, a warthog, or a **gazelle**.

Cheetahs have **marks** on their fur.

Their eyes spy **prey**.

Cheetahs balance with the help of a long **tail**.

# Photo Glossary

 **gazelle** (guh-ZEL): Fast, thin, hoofed mammal that lives in Africa and Asia.

 **marks** (marks): Stripes, spots, lines, or other patterns on an animal's fur.

 **prey** (pray): Animals hunted by another animal for food.

 **tail** (tayl): A thin part that sticks out from the rear of an animal's body.

# Index

African 3
cats 3
fur 4

hunt 12
legs 7
run 8

## About the Author

Lisa Jackson is a writer from Ohio. She would like to visit Africa someday, especially to see its amazing animals. For now, she likes to feed the giraffes at the Columbus Zoo!

© 2020 Rourke Educational Media

All rights reserved. No part of this book may be reproduced or utilized in any form or by any means, electronic or mechanical including photocopying, recording, or by any information storage and retrieval system without permission in writing from the publisher.

www.rourkebooks.com

PHOTO CREDITS: Cover ©johan1966; Pg 2, 11, 14, 15 ©Byrdyak; Pg 2, 12, 14, 15 ©edeag3; Pg 2, 6, 14, 15 ©Sarah_Cheriton; Pg 2, 4, 14, 15 ©mrisv; Pg 3 ©tankbmb; Pg 8 ©By JonathanC Photography / shutterstock; Pg 10 ©Byrdyak

Edited by: Keli Sipperley
Cover and interior design by: Rhea Magaro-Wallace

**Library of Congress PCN Data**
Cheetah / Lisa Jackson
(African Animals)
ISBN 978-1-73160-563-4 (hard cover)
ISBN 978-1-73160-449-1 (soft cover)
ISBN 978-1-73160-612-9 (e-Book)
ISBN 978-1-73160-686-0 (ePub)
Library of Congress Control Number: 2018967555

Printed in Ningbo, Zhejiang, China
05-0202512936